THE SECRET OF THE HIDDEN SCROLLS

BOOK ONE
THE BEGINNING

BY M. J. THOMAS

WORTHY
kids™

*For my wonderful wife, Lori, and amazing sons, Payton
and Peter. Thank you for your love and encouragement.*

—M.J.T.

ISBN: 978-0-8249-5684-4

WorthyKids
Hachette Book Group
1290 Avenue of the Americas
New York, NY 10104

Library of Congress Cataloging-in-Publication Data
Names: Thomas, M. J., 1969- author.
Title: The beginning / by M.J. Thomas.
Description: Nashville, Tennessee : WorthyKids/Ideals, [2017] | Series: The
    secret of the hidden scrolls ; book 1 | Summary: A scroll Great-Uncle
    Solomon, an archaeologist, found near the Dead Sea send Peter, nine, and
    Mary, ten, to the first moment of Creation and to the Garden of Eden.
Identifiers: LCCN 2017020346 | ISBN 9780824956844 (pbk. : alk. paper)
Subjects: | CYAC: Time travel—Fiction. | Creation—Fiction. | God—Fiction.
    | Adam (Biblical figure)—Fiction. | Eve (Biblical figure)—Fiction. |
    Scrolls—Fiction. | Brothers and sisters—Fiction. | Dogs—Fiction.
Classification: LCC PZ7.1.T4654 Beg 2017 | DDC [Fic]—dc23 LC record available
at https://lccn.loc.gov/2017020346

Cover illustration by Graham Howells
Interior illustrations by Lisa S. Reed
Designed by Georgina Chidlow-Irvin

Lexile® level 510L

Printed and bound in the U.S.A.
CW
15 14 13 12

CONTENTS

The Beginning

Peter waved as he watched his mom and dad drive away. Africa was a long way off, and a month was a long time. Especially when it meant staying with Great-Uncle Solomon.

"*Ruff!*" barked Peter's dog.

"You can't go, Hank," said Peter. "You have to stay here with us."

Hank whined. Peter wasn't happy either, but he wasn't going to show his sister, Mary, that he was trying not to cry. She never cried. She never even laughed much, come to think of it.

She was too smart and serious for that sort of thing.

Peter looked up at the huge house. Then he looked over at Mary. She shrugged and said, "We should go in now."

You would think she was five years older than him instead of just one.

"Okay," said Peter.

He opened the tall wooden door and followed her into a large room. Peter looked up at the high ceiling. His eyes followed the stairs up to a landing leading to the second floor. Mary looked at a large map on the wall. It had red thumbtacks stuck into every continent. Small stacks of books were scattered around the room, and an old compass sat on a table. Peter thought it looked more like a museum than a house.

Great-Uncle Solomon, their grandmother's brother, was sitting in a leather chair reading a book. He was short, with bushy, white hair and round glasses.

"He looks like Einstein," whispered Mary. "But he's probably not as smart."

All Peter knew was that his Great-Uncle Solomon didn't know anything about kids. The last time they had seen him, four Christmases ago, he had given them each a new toothbrush.

Hank ran past Peter and barked at a tall, shiny suit of armor standing at the entrance to a long hallway. It held a shield in one hand and a long sword in the other.

"Your parents didn't mention a dog," said Great-Uncle Solomon.

"His name is Hank," said Peter. "And he's the world's smartest dog."

"Really? Can he tell time?" said Great-Uncle Solomon.

"He sure can," answered Peter. "Hank, what time is it?"

Hank ran to the front window and looked at

the sun high in the sky. He ran back to Peter and barked four times.

Great-Uncle Solomon pulled out his pocket watch. "You are right, Hank. It is exactly four o'clock."

"He can also catch a Frisbee and play dead," said Peter.

"Impressive," said Great-Uncle Solomon. "Well, dinner will be served at five o'clock sharp. Hank, make sure they get to the kitchen on time. You kids can take a look around the house."

Hank ran over and barked at a scary wooden mask hanging on the wall. Peter picked up a rusty knife with a leather handle and a few coins with strange images on them.

Mary unfolded a dusty old map on a table. "Why do you have so many old things around your house?"

"Because I'm an archaeologist," Great-Uncle

Solomon said. "Do you two know what an archaeologist is?"

"Is it someone who decorates their house with old, breakable things, like my grandmother does?" said Peter.

"Not exactly," said Great-Uncle Solomon. "Mary, do you know?"

"Of course I do." Mary put her hands on her hips. "I'm ten years old. It's someone who travels to faraway places to dig up ancient artifacts and solve mysteries from the past."

"You're right," said Great-Uncle Solomon.

"That's what I meant," mumbled Peter. Of course Mary was right. She was always right.

Great-Uncle Solomon walked over to the large map on the wall and pointed at the red thumbtacks. "I have been all around the world and made many amazing discoveries." He pointed at one red thumbtack poked into China and looked toward Mary. "Like the one your parents made when they traveled to China and brought you home."

Mary gave Peter a look that said, *You heard that, right?* Then she said to Great-Uncle Solomon, "Where do you keep your discoveries?"

"I keep a few around the house, but the most important ones are in the library—down the hallway."

Peter ran down the long hallway past the suit of armor and stopped at the large wooden doors of the library. The doors looked twenty feet tall and like they were from a castle. Peter tried to open one, but he couldn't turn the large handle that was shaped like a lion's head. Hank barked and scratched at the doors.

"Not yet," said Great-Uncle Solomon.

"Why not?" asked Mary.

Great-Uncle Solomon shook his head. "I don't think you are ready."

"Ready for what?" Peter stood straight and tall. "I'm nine years old, and I can read."

"I'm sure you can," Great-Uncle Solomon said. "But there is much more than books in the library. Amazing things. Things you could only dream about." He paused and looked into space for so long that Peter thought he might have fallen asleep. "Well, enough about the library for now. I have to go make dinner." He turned and walked down the long hallway toward the kitchen.

Peter stood there and stared at the old library

doors. "One month stuck in a house filled with old stuff."

Hank kept barking.

"I hope he has a television around here somewhere," said Mary.

"I forgot to tell you, I don't have a television," Great-Uncle Solomon shouted down the hall.

"What have we gotten ourselves into?" said Mary.

"I just hope he's a good cook, because I'm starving." Peter headed off to find his bedroom.

2

An Amazing Discovery

Peter put his last pair of socks in the drawer and his suitcase in the closet. Then he lay down on the bed to test it out. As he stared at the ceiling, his stomach growled and his mind searched for something to do.

He heard Hank running down the long hallway, barking. "*Woof. Woof. Woof. Woof. Woof.*"

Mary poked her head out of her bedroom. "It must be five o'clock."

"Good." Peter slid off the bed and joined her. "All this boring stuff is making me hungry."

"It's not boring! It's very interesting." Mary led the way down the hall.

Peter rolled his eyes as he walked behind her. When they walked into the kitchen, they saw Great-Uncle Solomon pouring soup into three large bowls.

"Have a seat," said Great-Uncle Solomon. "We have lots of things to talk about."

Peter swallowed a big spoonful of the soup. It tasted like soggy cardboard and warm pond water.

"How does your soup taste?" asked Great-Uncle Solomon.

"It's good . . . I guess," said Peter.

Mary kicked him under the table and gave him a look. Peter reached down and rubbed his shin. Mary's karate training was really working.

Great-Uncle Solomon ate without saying anything. That seemed strange for somebody who had a lot to talk about. Finally, when Mary's bowl was empty, she asked, "What do you want to tell us about?"

"Come with me." Great-Uncle Solomon pushed himself back from the table and led them into the living room.

Peter could almost hear the old man's bones creaking. Mary and Peter sat on the big leather couch, and Hank lay down in front of the fireplace. Peter tried not to groan. This wasn't going to be fun.

"I have spent my life traveling around the world, and I've discovered many artifacts that prove the stories in the Bible are true," said

Great-Uncle Solomon. "But none of those discoveries compare to what I found one year ago on this very night."

"What was it?" Mary scooted closer.

"I haven't told anyone about this discovery yet," said Great-Uncle Solomon. "But I am getting old, and I think someone needs to know."

Peter sat up straighter. Maybe this wasn't going to be so boring after all. "You can tell us."

Great-Uncle Solomon stood up and quickly looked around the room. He checked under the pillows and behind the curtains like he was making sure no one else was in there.

"Who are you looking for?" said Peter. Who else could there possibly be?

"I think we're safe," said Great-Uncle Solomon.

"From what?" Mary looked behind the couch.

"Please don't interrupt," said Great-Uncle Solomon. He grabbed a safari hat and flashlight and sat down. "I was on a dig in the desert beside the Dead Sea in Israel. Did you know that anyone can float on the Dead Sea? You can lie right on top of the water like a boat. You can even roll on top of the water like a log."

"Was that your *amazing* discovery?" asked Peter. Okay, back to being boring.

"No, of course not." Great-Uncle Solomon stood up and put on his safari hat. He slowly walked across the room, looking ahead as if he was seeing something. Peter looked, too, but he didn't see anything.

"I was all alone one night when I found a tunnel that led to the middle of a big hill." Great-Uncle Solomon ducked his head and took two more steps. "It was very dark."

Great-Uncle Solomon ran to the wall and turned off the lights.

"My flashlight was losing power." He flicked his flashlight off and on.

"Why didn't you have one of those torches that don't go out?" asked Mary.

"That's only in the movies," said Great-Uncle Solomon.

Peter grinned. Maybe Mary didn't know everything after all.

Great-Uncle Solomon slowly walked across the room, pointing his flashlight straight ahead. "I could just barely see a door at the end of the tunnel. It had a large handle in the shape of a lion's head."

"You mean like the one on the library door that I couldn't open?" asked Peter.

"Yes. In fact, it was exactly the same," said Great-Uncle Solomon. "And just then, my flashlight went out and I was left standing in the dark."

"*Woof,*" barked Hank.

"No. *Dark*, not *bark*." Great-Uncle Solomon turned off his flashlight. "I reached into the darkness, grabbed the lion's head, and turned it. I pulled the door open and saw the most amazing thing."

"How could you see in the dark?" asked Peter.

"There was a large clay pot in the middle of the room, and it was glowing as bright as a full moon on a clear October night."

"What did you do?" Mary asked.

"I picked up the glowing pot, covered it with a blanket from my backpack, and ran back to my tent. There I discovered that the most amazing part wasn't the glowing clay pot. It was what was inside the pot."

"A pile of gold?" asked Peter.

"No, better," said Great-Uncle Solomon. "I found several ancient scrolls."

Peter crossed his arms and sat back. "How are scrolls better than a pile of gold?"

"After years of searching, I had finally found the Hidden Scrolls!" said Great-Uncle Solomon.

"Why were you searching for them?" Mary leaned so far forward that she almost fell off the couch.

"I spent many years in Israel and the Middle East digging and searching for artifacts to prove the events in the Bible are true. In my research, I discovered the Legend of the Hidden Scrolls. I knew I must find them."

"Why are they so important?" asked Mary.

"They are very powerful!" said Great-Uncle Solomon. "They can unlock the secrets of the past and prove the Bible is true."

"How?" asked Peter.

"Listen to the Legend of the Hidden Scrolls," Great-Uncle Solomon said. He cleared his throat and began:

THE SCROLLS CONTAIN THE TRUTH YOU SEEK.
BREAK THE SEAL.
UNROLL THE SCROLL.
AND YOU WILL SEE THE PAST UNFOLD.
AMAZING ADVENTURES ARE IN STORE
FOR THOSE WHO FOLLOW THE LION'S ROAR!

"What does that mean?" asked Peter. This was starting to get very interesting.

"The legend means that whoever opens the scrolls will travel back in time to the events of the Bible," Great-Uncle Solomon said.

"Why?" asked Peter. "What is in the scrolls?"

"I don't know. Each scroll has a red wax seal holding it together. Each seal has a different image pressed into it. I wasn't able to break the seals to open the scrolls."

Mary tilted her head. "Why not?"

"The legend of the scrolls goes on to say that only the chosen ones can open the scrolls. I guess I'm not one of the chosen ones." Great-Uncle Solomon took off his safari hat and slumped down on the couch.

"Let me try!" Peter shouted. "Maybe I'm one of the chosen ones."

Mary shook her head and rolled her eyes.

"I don't know," said Great-Uncle Solomon. "Only the lion will know."

"Who is the lion?" asked Mary.

"You will have to figure that out on your own," said Great-Uncle Solomon. "But right now, it is time to go to bed."

What? Go to bed with the scrolls hidden somewhere in the house? Peter was sure he'd never fall asleep.

3

THE LION'S ROAR

Peter awoke at midnight to what sounded like a lion's roar in the hallway. He shook his head. He must have been dreaming.

But Hank was barking in the hallway. Peter ran out to stop him before he woke everyone in the house.

Mary opened her bedroom door and rubbed the sleep out of her eyes. "What's going on out here?"

"I don't know. Hank won't stop barking," said Peter.

Mary looked across the hall and pointed. Peter followed her gaze. One of the doors to the library was cracked open just a little bit.

"Let's go in," said Peter.

"It's late, and we should be in bed," Mary whispered.

Peter walked toward the door. "Are you kidding? Don't you want to see all the amazing things in the library?"

"I don't think we're allowed to go in," said Mary.

"Great-Uncle Solomon never said we couldn't go in," said Peter. "He just said he didn't think we were ready, and something about a lion."

"I guess." Mary twirled a piece of hair around with her finger. "I *would* like to see what's in there."

Hank barked at the library doors again. Then he scratched at the cracked door, and it swung all the way open. Hank ran in before Peter could stop him.

Peter took off after Hank, with Mary on his heels. When he reached the middle of the library, he froze like a popsicle. Mary ran into him from behind. Peter rubbed his eyes. He couldn't believe what he was seeing.

The library was huge. Tall bookshelves went from floor to ceiling on every wall. He had never seen so many books in his life.

"Look at all these books," said Mary. "It's amazing."

"It's a lot of books," said Peter. "But where are all the cool things that Great-Uncle Solomon discovered? He said we would see amazing things that we could only dream about. The only things I see are books, and that's not a very good dream."

"Well," said Mary, "maybe he was just trying to make it fun for us."

"Or maybe he's not just old." Peter grinned. "Maybe he's old and crazy."

"I don't think so," said Mary. "Mom and Dad wouldn't have left us with a crazy person."

"*Woof, woof,*" barked Hank. He ran to a tall bookshelf on the right wall.

"What's he barking at?" asked Peter.

"I don't know," Mary said. "It seems like it's something on the bookshelf."

Peter walked over for a closer look

at the book Hank was barking at. It was a large book with a red cover. It didn't have a title, but a lion's head was painted in gold on the cover.

"Maybe this is the lion Great-Uncle Solomon talked about," said Mary.

"Hey," Peter said, "did you hear something that sounded like a lion's roar in the hallway a few minutes ago?"

"I did," said Mary. "But I didn't say anything because I thought I was dreaming."

Peter pinched his arm. "Ouch!"

"Why did you do that?" asked Mary.

"I wanted to make sure I wasn't dreaming," said Peter, rubbing his arm.

"Let's see what the book says." Mary reached down and pulled it from the shelf.

The tall bookshelf rumbled. Then it moved. It slid open to reveal a hidden room.

The room was dark except for a glowing clay pot sitting in the center.

Peter's jaw dropped. "I guess Great-Uncle Solomon isn't crazy after all," he said. "Let's go in."

Mary hung back. "I don't know about this."

Hank ran into the secret room, straight toward the pot.

"Hank, stop!" shouted Peter.

Hank dug his claws into the floor, but it was no use. He slid all the way across the floor and knocked the pot over. The scrolls fell out and rolled everywhere.

Mary gasped. "We better clean this up and get out of here before we break something."

Peter picked up one of the scrolls and looked at the red wax seal. It had a picture of a tree pressed into it.

"Hurry! We need to put them away before Great-Uncle Solomon finds us," said Mary.

As Peter went to put the scroll back in the clay pot, he tripped over Hank. He almost fell face first into the pot, but Mary grabbed it out of the way. Peter landed on the floor with a thud.

"Are you okay?" she asked.

"I am. But I'm not sure about the scroll."

Peter held up the scroll. The red wax seal was broken. Suddenly, the walls shook, books fell off the shelves, and the floor quaked.

Peter's heart pounded so hard he could almost hear it. When he looked at Mary, her eyes were round as soccer balls.

"Mary!" shouted Peter. He held the scroll in one hand and grabbed Mary's hand with the other. The library began to crumble around them. Then everything was dark . . . completely dark.

4

LET THERE BE LIGHT

"Who turned off the lights?" asked Peter.

"I can't see anything," said Mary. "I can't feel anything either."

"Everything is gone," said Peter. "No books, no library, no floor, no walls . . . no anything."

They were floating in the air, and it was completely dark and still. The air felt wet and slippery.

"Where is Hank?" asked Mary.

"Hank, where are you?" shouted Peter.

"*Woof, woof,*" barked Hank.

"He's over there," said Peter. "But how do we get over there?"

"I guess we could swim," said Mary.

"But we're not in water."

"It feels a little like water. Try kicking your feet and swinging your arms like you're swimming."

Peter swung his arms and kicked. He almost rammed into Mary, who was doing the same. He was glad nobody from swimming class could see him. It would have been pretty embarrassing.

Peter moved closer and closer toward the sounds of Hank's barking. He finally grabbed him. Hank licked Peter all over his face. Then they all just floated in the darkness.

"What do we do now?" asked Peter.

"I don't know," said Mary. "What does the scroll say?"

"I can't read it. It *is* completely dark, if you hadn't noticed."

"Well, I guess we just wait," said Mary.

They floated quietly for what seemed like hours.

"LET THERE BE LIGHT," said a big voice through the darkness.

A warm, beautiful light glowed everywhere. The darkness was gone.

Peter and Mary blinked and looked over at each other.

"Wow, that's bright," said Peter.

"I can see again," said Mary. "But even with the light, the only things I can see are you, Hank, and the scroll."

"Oh, I almost forgot the scroll." Peter started to unroll it.

31

"IT IS GOOD!" said the big voice through the light.

The light went away and the darkness rolled back in.

"How can it be good when I can't see anything?" said Peter.

"Now we can't read the scroll," said Mary.

They continued to float through the darkness. Peter was very tired. He could barely keep his eyes open. He heard a soft snore beside him and whispered, "Mary?"

She didn't answer. Mary was asleep and so was Hank.

The next thing Peter knew, he was waking up to the same bright, warm light he had seen the day before.

"LET THERE BE SKY TO SEPARATE THE WATER ABOVE THE SKY FROM THE WATER BELOW THE SKY," said the big voice.

The sky around them became clear. Peter looked down and saw nothing but water as far as he could see. He looked up from the water and over at Mary.

"Uh-oh!" said Peter. He quickly fell through the air and splashed into the water below.

"Swim!" shouted Mary.

"I am," said Peter. "But there's nowhere to go. There's nothing out here but water."

"Just keep swimming," said Mary. "It's our only hope."

"It's a good thing we had swimming lessons all those summers." Peter floated on his back.

"IT IS GOOD!" said the big voice across the water.

"It's *not* good," said Peter. "We are going to drown."

The water started getting rough. "I don't know how much longer I can stay above the water," said Mary. "And it looks like Hank is getting tired of dog paddling."

Peter pointed over the waves. "What is that brown thing way over there?"

"I think it's a boat." Mary waved her arms in the air.

A small wooden boat floated across the rolling waves. A large man wearing white reached out and pulled Hank out of the water. The waves grew rougher. He rowed toward Mary and pulled her into the boat.

"Thank you," said Mary. "Who are you?"

"I am Michael, and God has sent me to help," said Michael. The boat rocked back and forth in the waves.

"Hello!" shouted Peter. "Can I get a little help over here?"

The waves splashed in Peter's face, and he struggled to hold the scroll safely above the water. This was not the time for small talk. A crashing wave pulled Peter under the water. He kicked his feet and swam back to the surface.

Michael rowed toward him, but the waves pushed Peter away from the boat.

Michael held out the paddle. "Grab it!"

Peter reached for the paddle, but it knocked the scroll out of his hand. The scroll rolled and bobbed away across the waves. Peter let go of the paddle and swam for the scroll. A wave swallowed it into the deep water.

Peter dove into the darkness. Michael stood, spread his wings, and splashed into the water. Peter swam deeper and deeper, with Michael right behind him. Then Michael grabbed Peter by the arm, flew out of the water, and landed in the boat.

"You could have drowned!" shouted Mary. She sounded mad, but Peter could tell by the look on her face that she was glad he was safe.

Peter shivered and held up the scroll. "Look! It stayed dry."

"That was brave," said Michael. "Not very smart, but brave."

5

A MIGHTY FRIEND

"Thanks for rescuing us," said Peter.

"You can thank God for that," said Michael.

"How did God know that we needed help?" asked Mary.

"God knows everything," said Michael. "Besides, you are the only people right now, so I don't have much going on yet."

Mary tilted her head at him. "Who are you again?"

"I am Michael, an angel of God." Michael stood tall and spread his mighty wings. "I am the head of God's angel army, and I have been sent to protect you."

"What are you protecting us from?" asked Peter.

"I am here to protect you from Satan, the great enemy. He is another angel. He rebelled against God, and I helped kick him out of heaven." Michael held up a long sword that was as bright as the sun. "I have a feeling that he is going to try to mess things up here."

"Where are we?" asked Mary.

"You are on Earth. You are just a little early."

"What do you mean?" asked Peter.

"That is what you have to figure out," said Michael. "It's time to go over the rules of your adventure." Michael held up one finger. "Rule

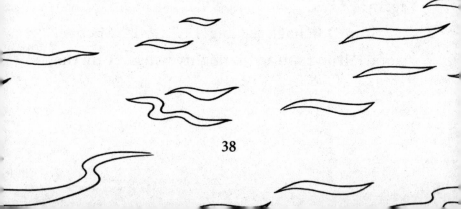

number one: you have seven days to solve the secret in the scroll or you will be stuck here."

"Stop right there," said Peter. "What do you mean by . . . stuck here?"

"You won't be able to go home. You will be stuck here forever."

"We'll never be able to see our family or friends?" asked Mary.

"That's right." Michael did not smile. He was very serious.

"That seems a little extreme." Peter felt his stomach rumble. He didn't know if it was from fear or hunger.

"I don't make the rules," said Michael. "Just solve the secret in the scroll and you can go home."

"Easy for you to say," said Peter.

"What's the next rule?" asked Mary.

Michael held up two fingers. "Rule number two: you can't tell anyone where you are from or that you are from the future."

"Who are we going to tell?" Peter asked. "There is no one else here."

"That's true," said Michael. "At least there's no one else . . . yet."

Mary leaned forward. "Are there any more rules?"

Michael held up three fingers. "Rule number three: you can't try to change the past. Now, let's take a look at the scroll."

Peter took out the scroll and unrolled it. The scroll had strange letters and symbols. Peter turned it sideways, upside down, and backwards. He couldn't read it.

Mary grabbed it out of Peter's hand. "Let me try." She squinted and studied the scroll. She couldn't read it either.

"The scroll is written in Hebrew," Michael said. "You have seven days to translate it."

"How are we supposed to do that?" asked Mary. "I know a little Latin and Chinese, but I don't know any Hebrew."

Peter rolled his eyes. How could she not know Hebrew? She knew everything else.

"You will have to pay attention," said Michael. "There will be clues for you along the way. Just be careful. You can't trust everyone or everything you will hear."

"How will we know what to believe?" asked Mary.

"Trust God, and remember what you have been taught. It's been a long day. Now it's time for you to go to sleep. You have a hard journey ahead." Michael spread his mighty wings and shot into the sky like a lightning bolt.

They were alone again, floating in a small boat in the middle of nothing but water. Suddenly it was dark again, like someone turned out a giant

light. Hank was already
snoring, and Mary's
eyelids were at half-
mast. Peter was too
wound up, but the
darkness and the
rocking boat finally
lulled him to sleep.

The next morning,
Peter was jolted awake
by the bright light again.

"LET THE WATER UNDER THE SKY COME
TOGETHER AND LET THERE BE DRY GROUND,"
said the big voice, across the water.

The water bubbled and swirled. The boat began
spinning. Peter held the scroll with both hands,
and Mary held on tightly to the side of the boat.

When the spinning stopped, the boat sat on
dry ground. Hank and Peter jumped out of the

boat and rolled around on the sand. Mary jumped out and kissed the ground.

"This is just like the beach," said Mary. "The ocean is that way and sand this way."

"I am starving," said Peter. "I haven't had anything to eat in three days."

"Me too," said Mary. "That bowl of soup wore off about two days ago."

"Let's go this way and look for food," said Peter.

They walked and walked and walked but found nothing besides more sand. Peter was so hungry that he picked up a pile of sand and thought about eating it.

"How long have we been walking?" asked Mary.

"I don't know," said Peter. "Hank, what time is it?"

Hank looked high into the sky. He looked up

and down, east and west, north and south. But he only whined and looked at Peter with his ears raised high.

"That's strange," said Peter. "Where's the sun?"

"I don't know," said Mary.

"Where's the light coming from?"

"From God, of course," said Mary. "Or maybe we just can't see the sun."

"IT IS GOOD!" said the big voice across the sand.

"How can it be good when we are so hungry?" asked Peter.

"LET THE EARTH GROW PLANTS AND TREES AND FRUITS AND VEGETABLES," said the big voice.

Grass began springing up. Trees sprouted from the ground. Fruit filled the trees. Splashes of bright colors filled the earth.

Peter grabbed a bunch of bananas from a tree

and ate and ate until he couldn't eat another bite. Mary picked apples, oranges, and broccoli. Hank dug up carrots and potatoes and ate them. Peter let out a huge burp.

"IT IS GOOD!" said the big voice across the green earth.

"Yes, it is." Peter rubbed his full belly and forgot all about the scroll.

6

One Starry Night

"LET THERE BE LIGHTS IN THE SKY TO SEPARATE DAY FROM NIGHT. LET THEM SHOW DAYS, SEASONS, AND YEARS," said the big voice across the green and blue earth.

Peter awoke when he heard the big voice. The bright sun hurt his eyes.

"I wish I had brought sunglasses," said Peter.

"I wish I had brought sunscreen," said Mary. "The UV rays aren't good for my skin."

Hank looked high into the sky and barked seven times.

"Hank can tell time again! It must be seven o'clock in the morning," said Peter.

"It's so nice to see the sun again," said Mary.

"Let's go down to the beach so I can work on my tan," said Peter.

"We don't have time for that right now." Mary pointed. "We need to figure out what the scroll says. It's already day four. We only have three days left, or we will be stuck here. Forever."

Peter unrolled the scroll. "How do we start?"

"I'm not sure," said Mary. "Michael said we need to look around for clues."

"It only has three words. It can't be too hard," said Peter.

"Maybe if you hold it up to the sun, we will be able to see the words in English," said Mary.

Peter held the scroll up in front of the sun. They stared and squinted, waiting for the secret message to appear.

"Do you see anything?" asked Peter.

"No," said Mary.

"Me neither." For once, Peter wished Mary were even smarter than she was.

"*Woof,*" barked Hank.

"Do you see something, Hank?" asked Peter.

Hank barked again and took off running. Peter ran after him, with Mary right behind. Hank was too fast for Peter to keep up, but he kept chasing. When he couldn't see Hank anymore, he followed his barks. Peter ran over the top of a hill and found Hank

49

walking toward them with Michael. The angel was eating an apple.

"This is delicious," said Michael.

"You like apples?" asked Peter.

"Is that what you call them?"

"Yes," said Mary.

"Then, yes, I like apples," said Michael. "I have never had one before."

"Is the apple a clue?" Peter said.

"No, it is a fruit," said Michael.

Peter shook his head. "No. I was wondering if it was a clue to help us solve the scroll."

"I knew what you meant." Michael laughed. "I was joking with you. Jokes were created long before the earth."

"Very funny." But Mary didn't laugh or smile. "We need help with the scroll. We don't have any of the words translated, and we're running out of time."

"I am here to help," said Michael. "Look for a clue in the sky."

"What kind of clue?" asked Mary.

"The first word of the scroll will be DECLARED to you as the sky turns dark tonight," Michael said.

"How will we recognize the clue?" asked Peter.

"Remember what you have learned, and look to the sky." Then Michael spread his wings and flew away.

Peter, Mary, and Hank spent the day enjoying the sun and all the delicious fruits and vegetables they could eat. They ran and played and waited for nightfall and for the first clue to be revealed. Finally, Hank looked high in the sky and barked seven times.

"It's seven o'clock," said Peter. "It's time for it to start getting dark."

"Let's sit down and watch," said Mary.

They sat quietly on the beach and watched the sky turn pink as the sun slowly disappeared.

"We just watched the first sunset," said Mary.

"What do you mean?" asked Peter. "We've seen sunsets at the beach before."

"No, I mean we watched the *first* sunset . . . *ever.*"

Peter looked up again. "Look at all the stars. I have never seen so many. It's like they go on forever. And the moon is shining so bright."

"Well, actually, the moon is not shining," said Mary. "It's just reflecting the light from the sun."

Peter rolled his eyes for about the fiftieth time. He already knew that. "I don't see any clues yet."

"Keep looking," said Mary. "What did Michael say?"

"He said the first word of the scroll would be declared." Peter thought for a second. "It seemed strange that he said the word *declared* so loudly."

"It reminds me of a Bible verse we learned," said Mary. "'The heavens *declare* the glory of God, and the sky shows the work of his hand.'"

Peter shook his head. Mary even had the Bible memorized. "So, are you saying that the stars and moon are showing us how amazing God is?"

"Maybe that's the clue," said Mary. "Is the first word *God*?"

The scroll shook in Peter's hand. He unrolled it. The first word on the scroll started glowing. The letters twisted and turned and changed into the word GOD.

"We solved the first word!" Mary did a happy dance.

"Well, *you* did." Peter didn't dance. "One down and two to go."

"IT IS GOOD," said the big voice through the star-filled sky.

"Yes, it is." Peter stared into the starry night and, once again, drifted off to sleep.

7

Swimming with Dolphins

"It sure is quiet." Peter took a big bite of banana for breakfast.

"That's true," said Mary. "I haven't heard any crickets chirping at night or any birds singing in the morning."

Peter looked around at the ground and the sky. "Now that you mention it, I haven't seen *any* birds or bugs or animals at all."

Mary looked around too. "I'm glad there are no bugs, but I do miss the birds."

"LET THE WATERS BE FILLED WITH FISH

AND GREAT CREATURES OF THE SEA, AND LET THE SKY BE FILLED WITH BIRDS," said the big voice across the ocean and through the trees.

The waters filled with swimming and jumping and diving creatures from shoreline to deep, dark ocean. The skies filled with colorful, flapping wings, and soaring songs echoed through the trees. The land and sea became alive.

"BE FRUITFUL AND MULTIPLY TO FILL THE WATER AND THE SKY," said the big voice to this new world of life.

"I didn't know that birds and fish could do math." Peter grinned at his sister.

"I think *multiply* means to have babies," said Mary seriously.

"I know." Peter rolled his eyes. "I was joking. Besides, they might be able to add and subtract, but there is no way they can multiply."

Mary paid no attention to him. Her face was

turned toward the sky. "Look at all the amazing birds. I have never seen so many colors and sizes."

Peter pointed high into the sky. "Look at that huge bird way up there."

Hank looked up and barked and turned in circles.

"That's not a bird," said Mary. "It's Michael."

"It sure is getting lively down here." Michael landed on the ground beside them. "Congratulations on translating the first word on the scroll."

"Where have you been since yesterday?" asked Peter.

"I have been trying to find Satan, the great enemy," said Michael. "I know he is up to something, but I am not sure where he is."

"Some people say he has horns and a forked tail, but I read that isn't true." Mary put her hands on her hips like she always did when she was about to ask a serious question. "So, what does he look like?"

"He could look like many different things," said Michael. "He could look like anybody or anything."

"So how will we know him?" asked Peter.

"You will know him by his lies. He will try to trick you with lies and turn you against God. It is best if you all stay together. It can be dangerous if you are alone."

"Don't worry, we will," said Mary.

"Remember, you will know Satan by his lies." Michael spread his wings and flew away.

"I am a little worried," said Mary. "What if we get tricked and don't solve the scroll in time?"

"Don't worry," said Peter. "You heard Michael. If we stay together, everything will be okay."

Mary still looked worried. "I sure hope you're right."

"Let's go down to the beach and see all the new sea creatures," said Peter.

"Okay, and maybe we'll find a clue," said Mary.

Peter ran down to the beach. He couldn't believe his eyes. He saw colorful fish, seahorses, starfish, turtles, and even whales. Then he saw something that took his breath away.

"Look at those dolphins jumping in the air!" he shouted.

"I read that a fully grown dolphin can jump twenty-five-and-a-half feet out of the water," said Mary.

"Let's get in the water and swim with them!"

"I don't think we can swim with the dolphins," said Mary.

"Why not?" said Peter. "They do at the water park."

"But we aren't trained," said Mary.

Peter ignored her. He jumped into the water and swam to the dolphins. When he looked back,

Mary was still standing on the shore looking nervous. He grinned. She might be smarter than him, but she wasn't as brave. Finally, she jumped in. But not Hank—he was too busy chasing birds on the beach.

The dolphins were very friendly. Peter swam and laughed and played tag with them. Mary petted one of the dolphins on the head and made squeaking sounds to communicate with them.

Peter heard Hank bark. He looked up and saw how far out he was in the deep water. Then he

saw something else—shark fins circling around them and the dolphins. Suddenly, Peter didn't feel so brave.

"Maybe they just want to play," said Mary.

"I don't want to wait to find out," said Peter. "Quick, grab the fin of one of the dolphins, and let's get out of here."

Peter grabbed the fin of the biggest dolphin. Mary grabbed the fin of the fastest dolphin. Peter shouted for them to swim and the dolphins took off. They were fast.

The only problem was that the dolphins were swimming in different directions.

Peter's dolphin swam straight for the shore, but Mary's dolphin swam out to sea. Peter stood on the beach and shouted, but it didn't help. Mary's dolphin kept swimming. The sharks kept following. Then they were gone.

Peter looked around and spotted the boat that

Michael had used to rescue them. He pulled it into the water. Hank and Peter jumped into the boat, and off they went. He had to rescue Mary. They had to stay together.

The waves were rough, but Peter kept rowing. They made it past the waves and shouted and barked for Mary, but there was no answer.

Peter kept rowing. His arms were getting tired and his hands were hurting. It was hopeless. Peter worried that he would never find Mary. He was afraid he couldn't solve the secret of the scroll by himself. And even if he could—what would happen to Mary?

"IT IS GOOD," said the big voice as the day ended and darkness covered the water.

"How can it be good when Mary is missing?" said Peter.

When he was too tired to row any longer, he drifted off to sleep in the boat.

8

Running with Rhinos

Peter woke to Hank's slobbery tongue licking his face. It was morning, and he needed to find Mary.

Peter rowed and called Mary's name. He rowed and rowed but couldn't find her. In fact, when he looked around, he couldn't see land either. All he saw was water. Peter was losing hope of ever finding Mary or getting back home.

Hank ran to the back of the boat and barked. Then Peter saw a dolphin swimming toward him. It swam in circles around the boat. Peter recognized it as the dolphin that had carried

Mary away. Maybe the dolphin could help. Peter started to feel a little hope.

"Do you know where Mary is?" Peter asked the dolphin.

The dolphin jumped into the air and swam away.

"Wait!" said Peter. "Don't leave us out here."

Peter rowed fast to catch up with the dolphin. It kept swimming and Peter kept rowing. Finally, Peter looked ahead and saw the shore.

This was not the beach they were on before. The dolphin had led them to a different beach. There were big rocks along the shore, and Peter could see tall trees in the distance, through a light fog.

"Maybe the dolphin brought us to where he took Mary," Peter said to Hank.

Peter jumped from the boat onto the beach. He was so happy to be on land again. But he was tired and hungry, and he missed Mary. He couldn't believe he actually *missed* Mary.

Hank ran down the beach and barked at something in the sand.

Peter ran to see. "What is it, Hank?"

Peter stopped dead in his tracks—a set of footprints in the sand. Peter put his foot beside a footprint. It was the same size as his.

"These must be Mary's footprints," said Peter. "Let's follow them. Maybe we will find Mary."

They followed the footprints down the beach. After about a hundred yards, the footprints changed direction and turned away from the

water. They disappeared into a garden that was as big as a jungle. The garden was green and full of fruit-filled trees. Two trees in the middle of the garden stood taller than the other trees.

"LET THE EARTH BE FILLED WITH LIVING CREATURES. LET BIG BEASTS AND CREEPING CREATURES COVER THE EARTH," said the big voice.

A mighty wind blew, and sounds filled the air. The land echoed with roars and growls and howls and squeaks. Hank barked and joined the chorus of creatures.

Peter was amazed but also a little scared. It sounded like there were some big animals in the garden, and Mary was stuck in there with them—alone. He had to go in to find her.

Time was running out. It was day six, and they only had one day left to solve the scroll. Peter's palms started to sweat, but he had to keep going.

Peter and Hank entered the great garden and searched for Mary. They found a river running through the middle. Peter and Hank both leaned down and drank the clear water from the river. Peter drank just like a dog.

"Let's walk along the river," said Peter. "Maybe Mary is thirsty."

Peter saw some banana trees and stuffed some bananas in his pockets for the journey. He heard a noise coming from behind the trees. He stood very still and quiet.

Crack!

A huge rhino trampled through the trees, squishing bananas and running straight at Peter. Hank stood in place and barked at the charging rhino.

"Run for your life!" yelled Peter.

"*Woof!*" barked Hank.

"*Snort!*" The rhino ran past Hank and charged at Peter.

Peter scrambled up a tree and held on tightly as the rhino rammed his big horn into the tree over and over again.

"Run, Hank!" yelled Peter. "Go find Mary!"

Hank disappeared into the garden. Peter's heart pounded. He was alone and in trouble. He couldn't figure out any way to escape.

Suddenly, a monkey jumped onto the branch beside Peter. The monkey jumped up and down like he wanted to play. He grabbed a banana out of Peter's pocket and threw it at the rhino. "Great idea!" He threw a banana too, but the rhino stayed put. "You're a funny monkey," said Peter. "Thanks for trying to help."

The monkey reached to grab another banana, but this time he pulled out the scroll.

"Give it back!" shouted Peter.

The monkey laughed and jumped to another branch.

"I'm not joking."

Peter jumped onto the branch beside the monkey and reached to grab the scroll. The monkey moved and Peter slipped. He caught the end of the branch and dangled right above the rhino's horn. The monkey jumped to another branch. Then he jumped to another tree. He jumped from tree to tree, disappearing into the distance.

"IT IS GOOD," said the big voice through the trees.

Peter looked straight down at the rhino's big, pointy horn. "How can this be good?"

9

A Slithery Snake

Peter's hands grew tired as he hung from the branch, inches above the rhino's horn. He tried to pull himself up, but he was too tired and scared.

Peter heard a rumble in the distance. The noise grew louder and louder, and the rhino ran away. The tree shook so much that Peter could barely hold on.

Something very heavy was coming. Peter saw a big cloud of dust. Suddenly, Hank ran out of the dust cloud. He was being chased by a huge herd of elephants.

"Run, Hank, run!" shouted Peter.

Hank barked and ran toward Peter hanging from the tree.

"No, Hank!" said Peter. "Run the other way. Those elephants will knock this tree over with me in it."

Hank didn't listen. He and the elephants headed straight toward Peter. Then Peter noticed someone riding on the back of one of the elephants. It was Mary!

"Stop!" yelled Mary.

All of the elephants stopped. Mary guided her elephant up beside the tree. Peter let go of the branch and landed on the elephant's back.

The rhino came back and played with Hank. They took turns chasing each other around the trees.

"Why were you just hanging around in that tree?" Mary gave him a look. "We don't have time to play around and climb trees. We only have one day left to figure out the scroll."

"I wasn't playing," said Peter. "I was trying to escape that huge rhino. He was about to trample me."

"No, he just wanted to play." Mary reached down to pet the rhino's head. "All the animals are friendly. They won't hurt you."

"I can't believe I'm saying this, but I am so glad to see you," said Peter. "But I have some bad news. I don't have the scroll."

"How could you lose the scroll?" Mary shook her head.

"I didn't lose it," Peter said. "One of those 'friendly' monkeys stole it and went that way." Peter pointed up into the trees.

"Which way?" said Mary.

"He was swinging toward the two tall trees in the middle of the garden," said Peter.

"Let's head for the trees and try to find that monkey."

"Well, if we are going to ride something, I'm going to ride the rhino," said Peter.

He grabbed the rhino by the horn and swung up onto his back. Peter steered the rhino, using its horn, and headed for the two tall trees. He wished his friends could see him now.

When they reached the trees, Peter jumped off the rhino's back and looked high into the tree on the left. It was full of amazing fruit. Something moved, but it wasn't the monkey.

A huge snake came slithering and winding down the tree. Its head was bigger than Peter's. Its fangs were longer and sharper than steak knives. It was hard to tell how long the snake was, because it kept wrapping around the tree, and Peter couldn't see its end. Its scales were shiny and reflected all the colors of the rainbow.

The snake was beautifully scary.

"Can I help you?" asked the snake in a deep, caring voice.

"A monkey stole our scroll, and we think he is in one of these trees," said Peter.

"I did see a monkey with a sssssssscroll go up this tree a few minutes ago," hissed the snake. "It seemed strange for a monkey to have a sssssssscroll. They are not the best readers."

"Can you go up the tree and get the scroll for us?" asked Mary.

"Well, of course I will," said the snake. "Anything to help friends."

The snake slithered up the tree and returned with the scroll.

"Where's the monkey?" asked Peter.

"You don't need to worry about the monkey anymore," said the snake.

Peter grabbed the scroll and examined it closely. It wasn't torn. It wasn't even smudged. He also wondered what might have happened to the monkey.

"Tell me more about the sssssssscroll," hissed the snake.

"We have to solve the secret of the scroll," said Mary. "Or we will be stuck here."

"Maybe I can help you," said the snake.

"*Woof.*" Hank stood in front of the snake, guarding Peter and Mary. The fur on the back of Hank's neck stood up.

"I don't think we should trust the snake," Peter said to Mary.

"You can trust me. I already helped you find the sssssssscroll," hissed the snake.

Mary nodded. "That's true. There are three words, and we already have the first word."

"What is it?" asked the snake.

"The first word is GOD," said Mary. "Do you know anything about God?"

"I know a lot about God," said the snake. "I know God hasn't been around here in a long, long time."

"Yes, he has," said Peter. "I just heard God in the garden this morning."

The snake stuck out his tongue and whipped it back in. "You couldn't have. God has nothing to do with this place or any of the creatures."

"That's not true." Mary pointed around the garden. "God made the world and all these creatures."

"You must be confused," said the snake.

"This world has always been here. God didn't make any of these creatures."

"Yes, God did," said Peter.

"How can you be sure?" asked the snake.

"I saw it happen!"

"That's impossible." The snake slithered closer to Peter. Hank ran at the snake and growled. Chills ran down Peter's back.

"Hank doesn't trust this snake, and neither do I," said Peter.

"I don't either," said Mary. "Because I know that God created—"

Just then, the scroll shook in Peter's hand. He opened the scroll. The second word glowed and changed into the word CREATED.

"Check it out, Mary!" Peter felt hope fill his body. Maybe they *could* solve the scroll. "We have the second word!"

"Actually, I did." Mary winked at him. "But

I guess you were part of it."

The snake was not happy at all. He revealed his sharp fangs. Before Peter could move, the snake wrapped around all three of them. Tight!

CREATED

"I think you three are here to ssssssstop my plan," hissed the snake. "And no one is going to ssssssstop my plan."

10

THE KARATE LESSON

The snake wrapped himself tighter and tighter around Peter, Mary, and Hank. Peter tried to get his arms free, but they were trapped in the snake's powerful grip. The snake was squeezing the hope out of Peter.

"It's no use," hissed the snake. "You cannot escape." The snake stared into Peter's eyes and showed his long, sharp fangs. "You have something I want. Now hand over the scroll, and I might let you go."

"You can't have it!" Peter wiggled in the

snake's grip. He pulled his arm closer to his body and tried to hide the scroll in his pocket.

The snake's head darted down. He grabbed the scroll out of Peter's hand with his sharp fangs.

"Give it back!" shouted Peter.

"Now let's see what's in this sssssssscroll." The snake released his deadly grip and slithered away from Peter and Mary.

"You have to give it back to us," said Mary.

"Or what?" asked the snake.

Mary opened her mouth but nothing came out. For the first time ever, she didn't seem to know what to say or what to do.

"Or..." Peter suddenly had an idea. "Mary will use karate."

"I don't know what karate is," said the snake.

"Well, you are about to find out." Peter looked at Mary and gave her a quick nod.

Mary ran straight toward the snake. She did

a front flip and jumped into the air with a spinning kick to the snake's mouth. The snake's head flew back, and the scroll flew into the air.

Peter ran and jumped over the snake into the air and caught the scroll. He turned around and threw it as far as he could.

A monkey was swinging from branch to branch. It jumped from the closest branch and reached for the scroll.

"Fetch, Hank," shouted Peter.

Hank took off like a lightning bolt. He jumped in the air and caught the scroll right before the monkey could grab it.

"Stay, Hank," said Peter. "Don't let anything take the scroll."

Hank stood still and made a low growling sound. The monkey slowly backed away. None of the other animals went near him.

The snake shook his head and rose up from the ground.

"So, that's what karate is," said the snake. "I will have to remember that."

The snake sprang toward Hank and the scroll. Mary jumped with another kick, but the snake slipped under it this time. The snake put another deadly grip around Peter, Mary, and Hank. It was much tighter this time. Peter's heart thumped faster and faster.

"I can hardly breathe," gasped Peter.

"Help!" shouted Mary.

A rushing wind whistled through the trees. Branches cracked and leaves swirled through the air. Michael the angel landed beside them and pulled out a big, flaming sword. Peter had never

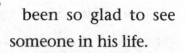

been so glad to see someone in his life.

"I knew I would find you, Satan," said Michael.

"You're too late," said the snake. He tightened his grip.

Peter couldn't take another breath.

"Release them now," said Michael. "They are not the ones you are after."

"Sssssssso what? I don't care who they are," hissed the snake. "No one will stop my plan."

Michael swung his flaming sword and struck the snake's head. The snake let go and made a terrible hissing sound. Peter fell hard to the ground. Hank plopped down in his lap. Mary landed beside Peter and grabbed his hand. They both stood and backed away from the snake.

The snake coiled tightly, showed his sharp fangs, and then darted straight at Michael. But Michael held out a large, shining shield. The snake's head smashed into the shield and he fell to the ground with a thud.

"I told you to leave them alone," said Michael.

"I will for now." The snake shook his head back and forth. "But they better hope I don't see them again when you're not around."

The snake hissed at Peter and slithered away, deep into the garden. Peter took a deep breath and let out a huge sigh of relief.

"Thanks for helping," said Mary.

"Great kick," said Michael. "You'll have to teach me how to do that someday."

"You saw the kick?" asked Mary. "Why did you wait so long to help us?"

"I was waiting for you to ask," answered Michael.

Peter grunted. "Well, that's good to know."

"If you're all okay, I have something amazing to show you."

Peter brushed himself off. "I'm good."

"Me too," said Mary.

Hank ran up and Peter took the scroll.

"Follow me," said Michael.

The four of them walked to the edge of the great garden.

"Stop here," said Michael. "We'll hide behind these trees. No one can move or make a sound."

"Why not?" asked Peter.

"He can't know you are here."

"Who?" asked Mary.

"No more questions," said Michael. "The time has come."

11

EVERYTHING IS VERY GOOD

Peter, Mary, Hank, and Michael stood silently behind the trees on the edge of the great garden. Through the mist, a glowing light appeared, hovering above the ground.

"LET US MAKE MAN IN OUR IMAGE, IN OUR LIKENESS," said the big voice from the glowing light. "LET THEM RULE ALL THE CREATURES I HAVE CREATED: THE FISH OF THE SEA, BIRDS OF THE SKY, AND ALL THE CREATURES GREAT AND SMALL ON THE EARTH."

The ground under the glowing light started to move and take shape.

The form of a man lay on the ground, breathless and motionless. The glowing light moved toward the man. The light touched the man's face, and breath flowed from God into the man.

The man took the breath deep, filling his body with life. He coughed and opened his eyes. He stared into the light.

He was alive. Peter couldn't stop staring. The first man was alive!

The man stood and walked into the garden with God.

"You can follow them," said Michael. "But you must not let the man see you. He can't see another human."

"We'll be very careful and quiet," said Mary.

"That was amazing," said Peter.

"This is only the beginning of the amazing things you will see." Michael spread his mighty wings once more and shot into the air.

"Where are they going?" asked Mary.

"It looks like they are headed to the tall trees in the middle of the great garden," said Peter.

"*Shh*. Don't talk so loud," whispered Mary.

They followed and hid behind trees. God and the man finally stopped between the two tall trees.

"YOU MAY EAT THE FRUIT FROM ANY TREE IN THE GARDEN," said God to the man. "BUT YOU MUST NOT EAT THE

FRUIT FROM THE TREE OF THE KNOWLEDGE OF GOOD AND EVIL. IF YOU DO, YOU WILL DIE."

The man nodded. This sounded familiar to Peter. There always had to be rules.

God showed the man around the garden. They talked and they laughed. It was like they were happy to finally be together. Peter thought it would be amazing to take a walk with God.

"IT IS NOT GOOD FOR MAN TO BE ALONE," said God. "HE NEEDS A HELPER."

The wind blew through the trees. The birds and animals seemed to be excited. They rushed to meet God's latest creation, the one God had made to rule and care for them.

The animals and birds gathered around the man. He named the animals. This took a while because God had made many animals.

"You are a *giraffe*," said the man

91

to the spotted creature with a long neck. "You, colorful, flying creature, will be named *parrot*. You look like a *turkey*. I name you three *monkey*, *moose*, and *mouse*. You are a *leopard* and you are a *gorilla*. You over there laughing, I name you *hyena*. You two, stop hopping for a minute. You are a *kangaroo*, and you are a *rabbit*."

The naming went on for a while. Peter looked around.

"Where's Hank?" he whispered.

"Look, he's out there with the other animals," Mary whispered back.

Peter looked and almost shouted out loud. Hank was running up to the man.

"Oh, no," Mary said. "Hank is going to blow our cover."

"It's too late," said Peter. "We can't stop him."

"I name you *dog*," said the man.

Hank danced on his back paws, then jumped

into the air and did a
back flip.

"You are one of the
smartest animals I have met,"
said the man.

"*Woof,*" barked Hank.

"I told you Hank was smart," whispered Peter.

Hank turned around and ran back to Peter.
The man finished naming all the creatures. He
was very creative with names. But suddenly
the corners of his mouth turned down and his
shoulders slumped.

"The man seems tired and sad," said Mary.

"I think he looks lonely," said Peter. "There aren't any other people."

"I think he needs a wife," said Mary.

"Of course *you* do," said Peter.

The man stretched out on the ground and fell into a deep sleep. The glowing light hovered over the man. God reached down and pulled a rib out of the man's side. Peter almost said, *Ouch!* out loud, but the man didn't even stir. The hole closed quickly and God took the rib off into the bushes.

"What's he doing?" Peter whispered.

"*Shh!*" Mary said. "Wait and see what happens next."

Peter heard leaves stirring. The man must have heard it, too, because he woke up. A woman walked slowly through the trees toward the man. The birds sang. The elephants trumpeted. The man ran to greet this beautiful new creature.

"You are bone from my bone and flesh from my flesh," said the man. "You will be named *woman* because you are a part of me."

"EVERYTHING IS VERY GOOD," said the big voice across the amazing creation.

"Yes, it is," whispered Peter. Suddenly he was very tired. He lay back against an apple tree and drifted off to sleep.

12

THE REST OF THE STORY

Peter woke to find Michael sitting across from him.

"What are you doing here?" asked Peter.

"Is something wrong?" Mary slowly sat up and rubbed her eyes.

"Not that I know of," said Michael. "But there will be if you don't translate the scroll today."

"I almost forgot," said Peter.

"Time passed so quickly," said Mary.

"I don't want to leave yet." Peter stood and walked a few steps away. He missed the rest of his family, but he also wanted to stay and explore God's wonderful new creation.

"The time has come," said Michael.

"Why is it so quiet?" asked Mary.

"It is the seventh day," said Michael. "God is taking the day to rest."

"I didn't think God could get tired," said Peter.

"He doesn't," said Michael. "But rest is a good thing. Now, you need to solve the scroll before it's too late." Michael stood and spread his wings.

"Goodbye," said Mary.

"Will we ever see you again?" asked Peter.

"I believe you will," said Michael.

Hank barked as Michael flew higher than they could see. They were alone again. It was up to them to get back home.

Peter worried they wouldn't be able to solve the last word. But he unrolled the scroll and sat down to figure it out.

"God created," said Peter.

"We already solved that part," said Mary.

"I know." Peter rolled his eyes again. "I am just thinking out loud."

"Maybe if we start listing all the things God created, we will find the answer," said Mary.

Peter had to admit it was a good idea.

"God created light," said Mary.

Nothing happened to the scroll.

"God created land," said Peter.

Nothing happened to the scroll.

"God created trees, grass, flowers, plants, fruits, and vegetables," said Mary.

Nothing happened to the scroll.

"God created birds, fish, animals, lizards, bugs, elephants, and rhinos," said Peter.

Nothing happened to the scroll.

"God created man and woman," said Mary.

Still nothing happened to the scroll.

Peter gave a big sigh. "I give up. This could take forever, because God created everything."

The scroll shook. The last word glowed and Peter watched it take shape. The word was—EVERYTHING. Peter's smile went from one ear to the other.

"You did it, Peter!" Mary started dancing. "You solved the secret of the scroll! GOD CREATED EVERYTHING."

"I knew it the whole time." Peter grinned at her. "I was just trying to give you a chance."

"Sure you were," said Mary. "What happens now? How do we get home?"

"I don't know." He was out of ideas. Peter rolled up the scroll.

Suddenly the scroll shook. The red wax seal fell off of the scroll and landed on the ground. As Peter bent to pick up the broken seal, it melted and transformed into something round and gold.

"A medallion!" Mary said.

"A what?" Peter said.

But he didn't wait for her to answer, because he noticed something. There was a tree on it, just like on the red wax seal. What was that about?

Peter didn't have time to wonder any longer. The ground began to shake. The trees swayed. Hank barked, and everything spun around them.

When the spinning stopped, they were standing in the middle of the library. Everything was just as it should be.

Great-Uncle Solomon opened the door and ran in. His hair was sticking out in every direction, and his eyes were bulging behind his glasses.

"What happened?" Great-Uncle Solomon asked. "A loud noise woke me."

"I'm sorry," said Mary. "And I'm sorry we were gone so long."

"What are you talking about?" said Great-Uncle Solomon. "You went to bed an hour ago."

"That's strange," said Peter. "I thought we were gone for seven days."

"What do you mean?" Great-Uncle Solomon asked. "What happened?"

"Something amazing." Peter held out the gold medallion inscribed with the shape of a tree.

"Where did you get that?" asked Great-Uncle Solomon.

Mary shrugged. "Never mind. You probably won't believe us."

"You never know," said Great-Uncle Solomon. "Tell me."

Peter unrolled the scroll and read the secret message. "GOD CREATED EVERYTHING." Then he told Great-Uncle Solomon about all the amazing things they had seen. He told him about Creation, the elephants, and Michael the angel.

Mary told him about the man and the woman. She told him how the snake tried to stop them and take the scroll.

"I can't believe it," said Great-Uncle Solomon.

"I knew you wouldn't believe us," said Mary.

"No, I mean I can't believe it's true!" Great-Uncle Solomon threw his arms in the air like he had just scored a touchdown. "I'm not crazy. The Legend of the Hidden Scrolls is true, and you are the chosen ones."

Peter gave Mary a high-five. It felt good to be the chosen ones.

"Don't get too excited," said Great-Uncle Solomon. "Being the chosen ones comes with a lot of responsibility, and there is much to learn. But we can talk about that later."

Peter's shoulders sagged. "I just wish the story didn't end."

"It was so perfect in the garden," said Mary. "All the creatures and the man and woman were so happy."

"That's not how the story ends," said Great-Uncle Solomon.

"What happened next?" Peter's shoulders straightened again.

Great-Uncle Solomon sat down in a leather chair and took out his big, red Bible. Peter and Mary sat on a soft, round rug in front of him. Hank curled up beside them.

"The story of Creation is found in the book of Genesis, chapters one through three," said

Great-Uncle Solomon. He told them how the snake tricked the woman and man into eating the forbidden fruit, how the man and woman broke the *one* rule God gave them. And then he explained that all of creation started to die.

"That's such a sad ending," said Mary. For once, Peter had to agree with her.

"That is not the end," Great-Uncle Solomon said.

He told Peter and Mary that God still loved the man and woman. Even though he kicked them out of the Garden of Eden and put angels in place to keep them out, God provided for their needs. Even though Satan and sin entered the world, God would forgive and fix everything someday.

Peter smiled. "I can't wait to find out how God does it."

"You will," said Great-Uncle Solomon. "Just be patient."

"Can't you tell us now?" said Mary.

"You will have to find out on your own," said Great-Uncle Solomon. "Now, go get some rest."

"But I'm not tired," said Peter.

"Go to bed," said Great-Uncle Solomon. "Rest is a good thing."

Peter smiled. He remembered Michael saying the same thing. He went to his room and climbed into bed with Hank curled up at his feet.

"You keep watch, Hank," Peter said. "And wake me if you hear a lion's roar."

Next time, he would know exactly what to do.

Next time . . .

Do you want to read more
about the events in this story?

The people, places, and events in *The Beginning* are drawn from stories in the Bible. You can read more about them in the following passages of the Bible.

Genesis chapter 1 tells the story of the six days of Creation.

Genesis chapter 2 tells about the creation of man and woman, the naming of the animals, and the Garden of Eden.

Genesis chapter 3 tells about the fall of man.

Revelation 12:7–9 tells the story of the battle between Michael and Satan.

CATCH ALL
PETER AND MARY'S ADVENTURES!

In *The Beginning*, Peter, Mary, and Hank witness the Creation of the earth while battling a sneaky snake.

In *Race to the Ark*, the trio must rush to help Noah finish the ark before the coming flood.

In *The Great Escape*, Peter, Mary, and Hank journey to Egypt and see the devastation of the plagues.

In *Journey to Jericho*, the trio lands in Jericho as the Israelites prepare to enter the Promised Land.

In *The Shepherd's Stone*, Peter, Mary, and Hank accompany David as he prepares to fight Goliath.

In *The Lion's Roar*, the trio arrive in Babylon and uncover a plot to get Daniel thrown in the lions' den.

In *The King Is Born*, Peter, Mary, and Hank visit Bethlehem at the time of Jesus' birth.

In *Miracles by the Sea*, the trio meets Jesus and the disciples and witnesses amazing miracles.

In *The Final Scroll*, Peter, Mary, and Hank travel back to Jerusalem and witness Jesus' crucifixion and resurrection.

ABOUT THE AUTHOR

 Mike Thomas grew up in Florida playing sports and riding his bike to the library and the arcade. He graduated from Liberty University, where he earned a bachelor's degree in Bible Studies.

When his son Peter was nine years old, Mike went searching for books that would teach Peter about the Bible in a fun and imaginative way. Finding none, he decided to write his own series. In The Secret of the Hidden Scrolls, Mike combines biblical accuracy with adventure, imagination, and characters who are dear to his heart. The main characters are named after Mike's son Peter, his niece Mary, and his dog, Hank.

Mike lives in Tennessee with his wife, Lori; two sons, Payton and Peter; and Hank.

For more information about the author and the series, visit www.secretofthehiddenscrolls.com.